The House
on Stink Alley

Also by F. N. Monjo

Indian Summer
The Drinking Gourd
The One Bad Thing About Father
Pirates in Panama
The Vicksburg Veteran
The Jezebel Wolf
Slater's Mill
The Secret of the Sachem's Tree
Rudi and the Distelfink
Me and Willie and Pa
Poor Richard in France
Grand Papa and Ellen Aroon
The Sea Beggar's Son
King George's Head Was Made of Lead
Willie Jasper's Golden Eagle
Letters to Horseface
Gettysburg: Tad Lincoln's Story
Zenas and the Shaving Mill
The Porcelain Pagoda
A Namesake for Nathan

The House on Stink Alley

A Story About the Pilgrims in Holland

by F. N. MONJO

illustrated by Robert Quackenbush

Holt, Rinehart and Winston
New York

dedicated to the memory of
George F. Willison
whose wit and scholarship
brought the Pilgrims so successfully to
life in his delightful book,
Saints and Strangers

Text Copyright © 1977 by F. N. Monjo
Illustrations Copyright © 1977 by Robert Quackenbush
All rights reserved, including the right to reproduce
this book or portions thereof in any form.
Published simultaneously in Canada by Holt, Rinehart
and Winston of Canada, Limited.
Printed in the United States of America
10 9 8 7 6 5 4 3 2 1

Library of Congress Cataloging in Publication Data

Monjo, FN
The house on Stink Alley.

SUMMARY: Young Love Brewster describes
the experiences of his family and other Pilgrims
living in Leyden in the years before the Mayflower
sailed for the New World.
[1. Puritans—Fiction]   I. Quackenbush,
Robert M.   II. Title.
PZ7.M75Ho   [Fic]   77-3469
ISBN 0-03-016651-9

Contents

1
The Saints from Scrooby

I am called Love, you must know, even though I am a boy. It is because Father is so religious that I was named Love-of-God Brewster. Now everyone calls me Love. I'm eight years old. Father has told all the members of our family that we are to call ourselves "God's people," or "Saints."

The whole company of us, here in Holland, are called Saints of the Holy Discipline, you see. All of us English exiles, who worship here in Leyden, in Pastor John Robinson's Green Gate meetinghouse, beside the quiet canal.

Father named my little brother Wrestling-with-the-Devil. He's only five. All of us— Father and Mother and Jonathan and my two sisters, Patience and Fear—we all call him Wrastle.

I do not think that Wrastle is at all meek enough to be a Saint, yet. Despite what Father says. But then I do not think that Wrastle thinks that *I* am meek enough to be a Saint, either.

Wrastle and I were born here in Holland, in the city of Leyden. But everyone else in our family came from England. Father and Mother used to live in a little country town called Scrooby, up in Nottinghamshire, halfway between London and Scotland. Mother told me that neither we Brewsters nor any other of the Scrooby Saints would ever have left England and fled to Holland, were it not for our wicked King James and his troop of wicked bishops. How Father and Mother hate those bishops! And how they hate King James! So does Pastor Robinson. And my brother Jonathan. And my two sisters. And William Bradford. And

FATHER   MOTHER   JONATHAN

Father's partner, Mr. Thomas Brewer. And all the rest of the English Saints who live in Amsterdam and Leyden. They all hate the bishops. And they all hate King James.

They're right to do so. For the King and his bishops are terrible, powerful men. Cruel, fearful, bloodthirsty men. And so we fear and hate them, for they would harm us if they could get their hands on us.

It was all because of them that Father and Mother and Jonathan and Patience and Fear had to run away from Scrooby.

All the Scrooby Saints had to try three times before they were able to escape from England. For twice, when they tried to reach the seacoast, with their children and their goods, they were caught by the King's bailiffs and sheriffs. They were stared at and jeered at by all the rest of the village folk. And then they were clapped

FEAR   PATIENCE   WRASTLE

in jail and fined and whatnot. King James was like the dog in the manger, in the fable: he did not want the Saints to be able to worship in their own way, nor would he allow them to live untroubled in Scrooby. But he did not want them to *escape* him, either!

William Bradford is only a few years older than my brother Jonathan. He grew up in Austerfield, near where Father lived, in Scrooby. Father was kind to him, because William Bradford was an orphan boy, living with his uncles, on their farm. And his uncles made mock of him, when he changed his religion, and joined the Saints, and came to worship in Father's posthouse, in Scrooby. He is just as kind to me and Wrastle, now, as if he were our own big brother. He married Mistress Dorothy, here in Leyden, and they have a son, John, who is just a tiny little boy.

W. BRADFORD DOROTHY JOHN

Father had told me much of the old times he saw, in England.

"Nay, Love," says Father, "I have not always lived in Leyden town, walking beneath the lime trees along the Back Canal! Teaching English to young blockheads at the University! I was once a secret messenger, for the Queen!"

It is true. Long before King James ruled England, when Father was a young man, he served old Queen Elizabeth. Father is now fifty-three, but when he was a lad of eighteen, he was the trusted messenger and body servant of Sir William Davison. And Sir William Davison was secretary of state for old Queen Bess.

Father visited Holland for the first time thirty-five years ago. The Queen had sent an English army overseas, to help the Dutch. In those days, Holland was at war with Spain, trying to win her freedom from the cruel Spanish king. The Spaniards had laid siege to Leyden then—to this very town where Wrastle and I were born!

Father told us all about that siege. How the Dutch broke the sea dykes. How they let the ocean flood the country round about Leyden, so that the Spanish soldiers had to flee! And how at last the Dutch could bring food into the town, for the folk in Leyden had been near starving for six months or more.

Many an evening when Wrastle and I are ready for bed, and we have said all our prayers, we ask Father to tell us about wicked old King James and his bishops. And often enough he will.

"Old Jamie's mother was Mary, Queen of Scots," says Father. "A kinswoman of Queen Elizabeth's. But Mary was a prisoner of Elizabeth's, all the same. A prisoner for many long years . . . until Elizabeth had Mary's head hewn from her body."

"Did she strike off Queen Mary's head herself with her sword?" says Wrastle.

"Oh, she did not kill her with her *own* hand," says Father. "Nor did Elizabeth allow herself to watch the headman's axe perform the bloody deed. But it was her hand that signed Queen Mary's death warrant. And did I not *see* that warrant, with my very own eyes? For was it not given to Sir William Davison, my master, for safekeeping?"

"When you were Sir William's secret messenger," say I.

And Father nods.

"Then, Queen Bess writes to Scotland," says

MARY, QUEEN OF SCOTS

KING JAMES I

QUEEN ELIZABETH I

Father, "to King James. For he was but King of
Scotland, then, and had not yet come to trouble
England. And good Queen Bess proposes this to
him, saying: 'If perchance your mother's head
be lopped off, Jamie, will ye be overmuch
angered with me? For if you should *not* be too
much disturbed, mayhap, in me will, I could
make you King of England.'"

"And what did King James reply to that?"
say I.

"Jamie replied," says Father, "that he would
not be too angry—seeing that his mother's life

13

was such a terrible burden to Queen Bess. And so Mary of Scotland must put on her taffeta dress of blood-red hue, and lay her head on the block. Aye, they said that her little lapdog shivered and clung to her skirts a long while. Long after her head was severed."

That story frightened Wrastle and me when we first heard it. But now we ask Father to tell it over, on many and many an evening.

"Now, in justice to the old English Queen," Father will add, "there is no doubt that Queen Mary, also, had been scheming to take Bess's life. For Mary had a hankering to sit on the English throne, herself. But once the Queen of Scots was dead, what do you suppose the Queen of England did?"

Here Father will pause, and draw a deep breath.

"Elizabeth pretended to fly into a rage with Sir William Davison! She was a crafty jade, was old Bess! She stamped and she swore and she cried out in anger. 'Sir William,' she roars, 'you have overstepped your authority! You have gone beyond my meaning! I gave that death warrant into your hands for safekeeping only! I had no mind nor desire that you should dare *use* it! Show me what commands you had from me, ordering Mary's death!' And poor Sir William knew not how to answer. For he knew—aye, all England knew—that Bess had wanted Mary dead. But now that her rival was safely buried,

TRAITOR'S GATE ~ TOWER OF LONDON

the old Queen had no wish whatever to *admit* what she'd done. So she had Sir William clapped in the Tower of London, as if the fault were *his*!"

"And did he never get out?" says Wrastle.

"Aye," says Father, "after a year or so, he was set free. After the huge Spanish fleet—the invincible Armada—had sailed into the channel. After we'd fought her and sunk her. After all that, did good Queen Bess set Sir William free. But during the worst of his troubles, I stuck by him and served him, all the while he was her prisoner, in the Tower."

"Then what happened, Father?" I will say, though I have heard the story often.

"Well, then," says Father, "my own father grew old, and ill. He that had been postmaster, up in Scrooby. And, when he died, I became postmaster there, myself, in his place. And I met your dear mother, and we were married. And Jonathan was born in 1593. And Patience, seven years after. And when Patience was but a little girl of three, old Queen Elizabeth died. True to her word, she left the kingdom of England to Jamie. And he rode down the Great North Road, from Scotland to London, so to be King of us all."

"Did you see him, as he rode down?" says Wrastle.

"Oh, aye! I saw him," says Father. "Trembling, slobbering, weak-kneed Jamie. For the Great North Road passes right through Scrooby, and we all saw him and his courtiers come trooping by. For a short time, there, we hoped he might prove kinder to us Saints than ever the old queen had been. But he was even more hardhearted than she. And he set his villainous bishops upon us."

Bishops! It always comes back to bishops! If it had not been for fear of the bishops, there would never have been any reason for the Saints of Scrooby to leave their peaceful homes in England. If it had not been for the bishops we never would have fled to Holland. And if it had not been for the bishops, again, there never would have been any reason for those dangerous books to be printed, in secret, in our house on Stink Alley.

2
King James and his Bishops

Here in Leyden, Father is the Ruling Elder of the meetinghouse which the Dutch call the Groenepoort, but which we call the Green Gate. Our pastor is the Reverend John Robinson. He and his wife, Mistress Bridget, have six children. They are James, Bridget, Isaac, Mercy, Fear, and Jacob.

The Green Gate is Pastor Robinson's home, but we use it on the Sabbath as our meetinghouse, as well. It stands on the Kloksteeg, which is to say, on Bell Alley. It is called Bell Alley because there the tall bell tower for St. Peter's Church stands, with the great church behind it.

Father told us that we must never speak of going to "church," for that is a word the *bishops* would like to have us use. Instead we must say "meeting," as do all the faithful Saints of the Lord.

Whenever we walk to meeting at the Green Gate, we can hear the Dutch singing hymns sweetly to the music of the great organ, in St. Peter's Church.

> *"A mighty fortress is our God,*
> *A bulwark never failing. . ."*

"Why can the Dutch have an organ, Father," says my sister, Fear, "when we must sing our psalms without one?"

"Nay, the organ is no better than the bagpipes of the Devil," Father answers, "and we Saints will never use one at our meetings."

How Wrastle and I do envy the freedom the

Dutch boys have! For when they have been to church, of a Sabbath morning, they are free, afterwards, to feast, or to go fishing, or to bowl on the grassy green. Or to fly kites. Or to sport about as they please.

But there is no feasting for us on the Sabbath. For we Saints believe that it is unlawful to cook on that day, or to do any work whatever but the work of the Lord. Sometimes, our noonday meal will still be lukewarm on the Sabbath, from the leftover warmth of the Saturday oven in which it was cooked. But it is forbidden to light a fire on the Sabbath. And Father forbids us to play all the games the Dutch boys play.

We wear clothes of gay hue, sometimes, during the week. But on the Sabbath, all of us put on dark blacks and browns and blues.

"Aye, sad colors, for Sabbath," says Mother. And this manner of dressing is much the same with all of us English Saints now living in Leyden.

All morning long, on the Sabbath, it is psalms and prayers and Bible-reading. And more of the same in the afternoon.

This is the way we dignify our meetings: all the men sit on one side of the aisle, the women

on the other. All the children are grouped together, under the eye of the elderly deaconess. She has a birch rod, with which she strikes us whenever we are sleepy or noisy. Thus she keeps us quiet and wakeful.

Pastor Robinson always wears black clothes and black gloves for the services.

Sometimes, of a Sabbath evening, Father will talk to us of the meaning of Pastor Robinson's sermons. Other times he will tell us of the persecutions and troubles which came to the Saints in England, because of King James and his bishops.

"Love," says Father, "when you and Wrastle shall be able to read your Bibles entire, from cover to cover, you will find that there *never* were any bishops in Galilee, when Christ had his ministry there. King James's church has lost its ancient purity. And we Saints would cleanse it, and restore it, to the way it used to be."

It is hard for Wrastle and me to understand these matters. For the Bible is a great, thick book, and difficult of understanding. I wonder when, if ever, I shall have read it all.

"Tell the boys, Father," says Jonathan,

"something of church government, that they may know the cruel ways of King James and his bishops."

Then Father will explain that there are *three* ways to govern a church. One is King Jamie's way, with bishops chosen by himself. Then these same bishops will choose all the pastors—the ministers who will serve every church in every hamlet and town throughout the whole country.

"This makes the bishop a *tyrant,* in England," says Father. "For is his word not law? All are forced to go to his services there—even we Saints must attend. Even we who *know*—from what we have read in our Bibles—that all of his churches must reform and submit themselves to our Holy Discipline. Aye, they must reform and *cleanse* themselves, if they would follow the word of the Lord! The bishops must be cast out, and in their stead there must be pastors and teachers and deacons—of the people's own choosing—just as *we* now order these matters, in the Green Gate meetinghouse."

It is not easy for Wrastle and me to understand everything that Father says.

"In England today," says Father, "all must worship ministers that King James and his bishops have chosen. Even though this is *not* the godly way."

The two of us try to listen carefully to Father, but often we grow sleepy. But who could fail to see how strongly he feels the need for these reforms and changes? Still, it is difficult to follow what he says.

Father tells us, next, of the *second* way the church might be governed, as it is in Scotland, where they have no bishops, but Elders instead. Presbyters, they call them. A council of Presbyters, or Elders, for each church, watching over its welfare.

"There is more liberty, in groups of this kind," says Father, "than there is with a single bishop. For the councils of Elders are many, and a bishop is but one man. And yet, there is a *third* way. *Our* way. Where every man in the congregation has a voice in choosing his pastor. We Saints of the Holy Discipline insist upon having *forward* ministers, of our own choosing. Men who know the Bible and the word of God. That is the way it is with us, Love, here in Leyden. And for the reason that we hold firmly to our beliefs, stiff-necked and stubborn as we are, King Jamie hates us. And has made us flee from our homes."

"Why should he fear our ways so much?" I ask him.

"They shake his authority," Father answers, with a grave and sorrowful air. "King Jamie would have us believe that he himself is a god, set up over us by Jehovah himself. No man may contradict Jamie's will, lest Jamie fly into a slobbering, shaking rage. Why, when he was first come into England, as King, out of Scotland, eight hundred of our forward preachers begged him to tear the hands of his bishops from off the throats of our congregations. Begged him to let us Saints choose our *own* ministers."

"And what did King Jamie say to that?" I ask him.

"He went into one of his rages," says Father. "'I will none of *that*,' cries Jamie. 'No bishop, no *King!* Away with all your snivelling! I will *make* ye conform, or I will harry ye out of the land!'"

Wrastle and I sit there, looking at Father in silence.

28

King James and his Bishops

"Now it is a fearsome thing," says Father, "to be hauled into some wicked bishop's court. For a bishop can hang a man, if he pleases. This is what some of them did to three of my old school friends. Three who went to college with me, in Cambridge, back home in England, many years ago."

"Did the bishops hang them, Father?" says Wrastle.

"That they did, and worse. John Penry, John Greenwood, and Henry Barrowe. All of them Saints of the Lord, like us. All of them wanted the church made pure. Wrote books to that end, and printed them in secret. Smuggled them everywhere, hand to hand. Until they were caught, and flung into jail. Thrown into the clink to rot, until they were tried and sentenced. And then condemned to be hanged, and drawn, and quartered. Hanged! And then cut down from the gallows, before they were even half dead. The breath not yet out of their bodies. Then their bellies were cut open, and their guts drawn out, as you would clean a fowl. And their bowels burned, before their very eyes. Burned by the reverend bishops' hangman! *That* is what your bishops can do! And that is why we *hate* them!"

Father's face is ashen when he finishes the telling. And when Wrastle and I finally fall asleep, we wake again with bad dreams. Dreams of bishops and books and hangmen.

3
The Midnight Setting of
Perth Assembly

Father—William Brewster—is much more than just a tutor at the University here in Leyden. He is also our Ruling Elder, as I have told you. And there is even more to tell. He has begun printing books. Church books. And some of them are bitter against the bishops, and against King James.

Wrastle and I aren't supposed to know. It is a very dangerous and secret business. Father would be in terrible trouble if ever the bishops were to find out what he is doing. Or if the Dutch were to know. Or wicked King James!

It is no wonder that Mother and Patience whisper together so much of the time, and sigh, and shake their heads.

One of the Saints, here in Leyden, Mr. Thomas Brewer, is in this thing with Father. He is helping him print these books, in secret. He and Father have brought two men over from England who know how to set up type. The master printer's name is John Reynolds. His apprentice is Edward Winslow. Mr. Reynolds and Mr. Winslow work downstairs, in the cellar, at night, when they think Wrastle and I are asleep. But sometimes we creep downstairs. And we hide ourselves in the shadows, in the passage. And we hear what they're saying!

The type that Mr. Brewer is using is called Roman. And here is what Father's name would look like, if it were set in that Roman type:

ELDER WILLIAM BREWSTER

And here is the way his name would look if it were set the same way they usually print their books, in Holland:

𝕰𝖑𝖉𝖊𝖗 𝖂𝖎𝖑𝖑𝖎𝖆𝖒 𝕭𝖗𝖊𝖜𝖘𝖙𝖊𝖗

The second type is called "black letter." Sometimes they call it "Gothic." It looks nothing like Roman type. We English folk think Roman is easier to read—but it is that Roman type that has got Father and all of us Saints into fearful trouble!

A year ago, in 1618, King Jamie called all his Scottish ministers together. He made them all come to the city of Perth, and there he had his bishops tell them that he would not allow them to rule their Presbyterian churches any longer by means of their Elders. From then on, all the churches in Scotland must be ruled by none but King Jamie's bishops. All the forward preachers of Scotland must bow to the rule of those hated bishops. Bow to their rule, or be punished!

Father was angry and sad when he heard it. And now, I am old enough to understand why. For was not King Jamie busily robbing the Scottish church—and the Scottish people, too—of their rightful liberty?

One of the bravest of all the Scottish ministers—the Reverend David Calderwood—was then in hiding, near Perth. King Jamie had had him in prison once before, so Calderwood dared not be caught again.

But when Dominie Calderwood learned what

the bishops had done, at Perth, he was furious with them. And furious with King James. So he wrote a book—an angry book—which he called *Perth Assembly.* In it, he said that everything that the bishops had done at that meeting—*all* of it—was worthless. The Scottish church must pay no mind to that illegal meeting in Perth, he wrote. They must go on being ruled, as always, by their Elders. And they must pay no mind whatever, he said, to any of King Jamie's wicked bishops.

A handwritten copy of his book was smuggled out of Scotland. It was sent to Father, here in Leyden. And it is this very book that Mr. Brewer and Father are having set, in Roman type. Here, in our house on Stink Alley!

Father and Mr. Brewer have printed quite a few books here, on the Stincksteeg—as Stink Alley is called in Dutch. On those books which will not make King James too angry, he has printed his name and address, in Latin.

Here is the way they read:

Lugdunum Batavorum
Apud Guiljelmum Brewsterum
in Vico Chorali
MDCXIX

The Midnight Setting of Perth Assembly

Had it been printed in English, it would have read:

Leyden, Holland
published by William Brewster
in Choir Alley
1619

Father doesn't ever let it read: Stink Alley. The house is L-shaped, with its main entrance on the Stincksteeg. But there is also a small side entrance on the Koorsteeg—on Choir Alley. So Father always has his books printed under that sweeter-smelling address.

But he and Mr. Brewer have dared put no name or address whatever on Dominie Calderwood's dangerous *Perth Assembly*. On *that* book, nothing is to be seen but the date: MDCXIX. For they are sure that, in England, the king and his bishops will be certain to find it a hateful and dangerous work.

Father couldn't have Mr. Reynolds and Edward Winslow print it at our house. For we have no printing press of our own. There is nothing here but the trays of type and the metal forms for locking up the pages. Mr. Reynolds and Edward Winslow have set the book carefully, line by line, and have broken it up into pages. When a batch of pages is ready, they send them out to a nearby printer, and those pages are run off. Then the type comes back, and they break it up, distribute it, and use it again for more pages. And so the work goes on.

Mother and the girls are terribly worried that someone will discover what Father is doing. Even Jonathan and Wrastle and I fear what King James may do, if he should find out. We know that King James has a long arm, which can reach over the sea, even into Holland, if he grows angry enough. For the Dutch are badly in

need of his help. There is nobody else but King
Jamie to help shield them from their old enemy,
Spain, should war break out again. And so the
Dutch have to keep seeking to please him.

Now that Dominie Calderwood's angry book has at last been printed, Father and Mr. Brewer say it must be sent over to Scotland at once. For what is the use of hatching a hornet, if nobody gets stung?

Yet *Perth Assembly* cannot be shipped by ordinary means. A crate of Saintly books from Leyden would be seized and broken open and burned by the King's men the moment it landed on the docks in Scotland. So, Father has thought of a wonderful disguise. All copies of the book will be packed into brandy kegs and wine casks. Wrastle and I have been watching the work, in the shadows, late at night, while the candles gutter and flicker.

Father and Mr. Brewer and Jonathan and Mr. Reynolds and Edward Winslow have been working late, busily packing books into barrels. Sometimes Mother and Patience help, too. Then the barrels are headed, and hooped, and stacked—so that when they are rolled out onto the docks in Scotland, King Jamie's customs men will think them nothing but tuns of claret or Burgundy or fine French brandy. Though they are full to the brim with stuff far stronger than any brandy or wine!

41

4

The Long Arm of King James

In the spring of last year, in April, Father told us he must himself go to London. Patience and Fear and Jonathan and Wrastle and I were surprised to learn that, for once, it had nothing to do with bishops!

It had to do, instead, with his fear of a coming war with Spain. For the Dutch had a twelve-year truce with King Philip III of Spain—but that truce period was now fast drawing to its close. And the Dutch feared that war would break out as soon as the time was up.

The Dutch beat their drums and went out into the streets. They spoke of recruiting another army. There was frightened talk that Leyden might see another Spanish siege, worse

43

than the starving time they had seen forty-five years before.

The older men amongst the Saints were worried to think that some of our young men might volunteer for soldiers, if the Dutch should go to war. They worried, too, to see some of us children falling away from the holy discipline of the Saints of the Lord—and some of us young folk growing up more Dutch than English.

Pastor Robinson and Father and the heads of many other families of Saints often talked of yet another removal, of all of us, to a place of greater safety.

"We might think of planting in Guiana," said Pastor Robinson.

"Or even in Captain John Smith's Virginia," said Father. "For he has offered to guide us there, or to New England. For a fee."

"Captain John Smith might be of good help to us," said Pastor Robinson. "But since we have little enough money, his maps will be much cheaper than he."

So Wrastle and I would hear them arguing for this place and that. For a time, they talked of removing to the Dutch colony in New Amsterdam.

"It is not as if we would leave much of the

world's goods behind us, here in Leyden,"
Father would sigh. And it was true, for most
Saints are poor indeed, working hard from
dawn to dusk, at looms in the weavers' trade.

For all these reasons, there were many who
wished to leave Holland for the New World.
And great numbers of the Saints of the Holy
Discipline turned to Father to help them
borrow the money that would be needed for
ships and supplies.

So Father agreed to make the dangerous
voyage to London to plan for the trip. He left
Mother and the rest of us here in Leyden.

I remember Mother weeping, sometimes. For
she knew that if we decided to remove, Jonathan must stay behind in Leyden, with the
girls. For there would be only money enough for
her and Father and Wrastle and me to sail for
that wild plantation on the other side of the
wide gray ocean.

When we were in our beds at night, Wrastle
and I would talk of the feathered men, the Indians, who live there in the forests. We have
heard fearsome stories of them, and of what
they may do. We were frightened. And yet, if
Mother and Father were venturing there, we
wanted to go with them.

Still there was talk of war with Spain. And yet the lime trees flowered along the peaceful canals. Holland had never seemed richer nor quieter nor more secure. While New England was far, far away, and unknown to us all.

Father had dared to venture into King Jamie's London, for he was trying to draw up an agreement with some wealthy men there, so that we Saints could sail. I remember hearing of arguments and angry letters, back and forth. Of promises broken. Talk of charters and ships and money. I did not understand the half of what I heard, but I knew we were uncertain whether we should stay in Leyden, or sail away. And I knew that Mother kept weeping and worrying much.

She had much to weep for. There was great danger for Father in London. Soon after he went there, Pastor Robinson had a letter from England telling us that copies of *Perth Assembly* had been discovered and read by King James's bishops. Then we heard that King James had begun to suspect that the books were being printed in Holland. He and his men were hot to find out just *where*. And to learn by whom they were written. And to have the names of

the men who had printed them! Poor Father might be hanged for what he had done!

Mother told us that Father would have to go into hiding. "But you must tell *nobody!*" said she.

Mother thought Father might hasten to Scrooby, where the Brewsters used to live, and where he still had some good friends who would keep him safe from the King. But he no longer dared write to us. And so we could learn nothing further of how he was faring.

47

Mr. Brewer took great fright when we all heard that a search had begun in Holland, to find out where *Perth Assembly* had been printed. He told John Reynolds and Edward Winslow to pack up all the printing type, downstairs. Then he had everything carried off to his own house, on the Kloksteeg. There he hid the trays of type in his attic.

Now there was no doubt whatever that the long arm of wicked King Jamie was reaching across the sea into Holland! Wrastle and I were frightened. The King's ambassador to Holland, Sir Dudley Carleton, threatened the Dutch officials in Amsterdam and in Leyden. He said King Jamie would never send help if Spain should go to war with Holland, unless Holland would help search out the English criminals who had printed *Perth Assembly*. King Jamie wanted to question the printers, he said, in Whitehall Palace in London!

I remembered everything Father had ever said about how much King Jamie hated the Saints. Father had told me how the King, in one of his red-faced, slobbering rages, had said that he wished he could get his hands on every Saint and Presbyterian in both his kingdoms of England and Scotland! He wanted to see *all* of them cut into collops, and cast into Hell!

Pastor Robinson came to our house on Stink Alley and prayed with Mother, when he heard of Father's new danger.

Then, one night in July, Dutch bailiffs beat on our door, and forced us to open. They searched the house from cellar to attic, looking for Roman type, like that which had been used

in printing *Perth Assembly*. They found nothing in our house, for Mr. Brewer had moved it all to *his* house. But we were terrified to see that King James and his bishops had traced the book—just by the look of its type—right to our house on Stink Alley!

The Dutch bailiffs arrested Mr. Reynolds that night, mistaking him for Father. They let him go next day. Mr. Reynolds said the bailiff was but a drunken fool, yet how frightened all of us were that night, and in the days that followed!

In August, Dominie Calderwood himself left England, and fled to our congregation at the Green Gate, in Leyden. How odd it was, and how fearsome, to think of him hiding in our midst, praying with Pastor Robinson on the Sabbath with all the rest of the Saints. The author of *Perth Assembly,* hiding in Holland! And Father, its printer, hiding somewhere in England!

We asked Dominie Calderwood if he had any news of Father, but he had none.

Imagine our surprise and our terror when we learned, soon after, of Mr. Brewer's arrest. That same drunken bailiff and his men had gone to his house to search it, just as they had searched ours. They *found* the trays of Roman type, in his attic! By comparing them carefully, letter for letter, with a copy of *Perth Assembly,* the Dutch authorities were soon positive that Mr. Brewer's types had printed that dangerous book.

The bailiff's men seized all Mr. Brewer's books and papers and types. They nailed the door of his attic fast, and sealed it up with green wax seals.

Mr. Brewer was flung in jail. And King James's ambassador, Sir Dudley Carleton, demanded that he be sent at once to London. From September to December the Dutch wrangled with Sir Dudley. They did not *want* to let the English have Mr. Brewer, for they feared King James might harm him.

But King James blustered and threatened. He promised the Dutch that he would do no worse than *question* Mr. Brewer. So at last they gave him up, and he was sent to London.

Later, Mother was told that the King raved at Mr. Brewer, demanding to know where Father was. And Mr. Brewer himself raved and rambled, as if he were quite mad. They say the King could make but very little of him, and called him a fantastical fellow.

Mother and Wrastle and Jonathan and the girls and I could have kissed Mr. Brewer's feet, for all his bravery in this business. For we thought he knew where Father was hidden, and he might very well have told the King, to save himself. And yet he did not.

These were the events of a year or so ago. The terrible year of 1619. We moved in with the Robinsons. The house on Stink Alley was left dark

and sad and quiet. We received one single message from Father, saying that he was well. But there were no letters at all.

Early this spring we learned that the Saints and the businessmen were still wrangling, in London, over the terms of our removal to New England. First they said we might own the land where our houses would stand, and where our garden lots would be planted. Then it was no, we might not, and our houses and gardens must belong to the company that would furnish us the money to plant in New England. Thus it went, back and forth, this past March and April and May.

Father sent word that only Mother and Wrastle and I were to sail, if all could be arranged. Jonathan must stay with Patience and Fear, in Leyden, as had been decided before, until there was money enough to bring them over. Pastor Robinson and his family would not be sailing, either, for most of the Saints would remain in Leyden, and they would have need of him.

In June we were told that a small vessel of sixty tuns burden had been secured for our passage to America. First we would sail to Southampton, England, with forty-six of us Leyden Saints, together with firkins of Dutch butter, and flour, and beer, and cider, and barrels of salt beef, and codfish, and other necessaries for our voyage.

Mother told us that once we arrived in England, Father would have to slip on board as a stowaway! For King James was still hunting him!

At last, all was ready. Our chests were packed and sealed and tied with rope. Our smaller belongings were stuffed into bundles and sacks. Jonathan and the girls would move in with Pastor Robinson, at the Green Gate.

Our house on Stink Alley was put up for sale.

Young William Bradford and his wife, Mistress Dorothy, sailed with us on the *Speedwell*. For that was the name of our ship. How sad Mistress Dorothy was that her little son, John, who is only five, was too young to come with us. He has had to stay behind, too, with the Robinsons, at the Green Gate.

Mother told us that there would be a second ship, waiting to join us in England, carrying another party of English Saints, who were ready to sail with us to the New World.

Will I ever forget the day we departed? It was

the last of July, in 1620, when we boarded the canal boat. It was taking us down to Delfshaven, where the *Speedwell* lay. It took us eight hours to make the journey. We passed through Ryswick and then through the city of Delft, and so to Delfshaven. Jonathan and Patience and Fear came with us. So did all the Robinsons, and many, many of the Saints from the meetinghouses in Amsterdam and Leyden, to bid us farewell.

We lay that night on shipboard. Next morning, Pastor Robinson wept and prayed for our safety, on the deck of the *Speedwell*. It was terrible sad to hear little John Bradford cry, when he found that his mother and father were leaving without him. Then the rest of us wept and embraced and prayed and parted—not knowing if we should see one another ever again in this life.

*   *   *   *   *

It was an easy sail from Holland to Southampton, where the other ship lay. She is called the *Mayflower,* and she is three times larger than the *Speedwell.* For the *Mayflower* is ninety

feet long, and her deep hold is all of eleven feet, down to the keel. They say she is only twelve years old, and she is what the sailors call a "sweet ship," too, for she has been used only in the Portugal wine trade, and so she does not stink of fish.

All we wanted was a sight of Father, to know that he was safe. And indeed, after nightfall, he came aboard the *Speedwell,* by stealth. Mother wept. And Wrastle and I could see that there was much more gray now, in his hair, and in his beard.

Twice, in August, our two ships put out to sea, heading for the New World. But both times we had to put back to shore, for the *Speedwell* was leaking so hard we feared she would sink. She could not be repaired.

At last we had to abandon her, and crowd aboard the *Mayflower.* There was not room enough for all of us who wanted to sail, and some had to be left behind. There's one hundred and two of us, now, on board, not counting the sailors.

We are sad to be leaving so many of the Saints behind us, in Holland. But Mother is so glad to have Father safe with her, out of the hands of King James and his bishops, that she smiles when others are weeping.

Father promises that we shall have no more to fear from King James and his wretched bishops once we reach New England. We shall have our own forward preachers, and they shall be of *our own* choosing! And we shall worship God, in our meetings, just as we please.

Today is September 6, 1620. We are sailing west, toward the setting sun. It is a two months' journey, they say, across that wide, gray ocean. And there are many dangers ahead, of that we may be sure. But we Saints have our courage. And the Lord will provide.

The End

About this Story

This is historical fiction, for nothing is known of
what young Love Brewster actually saw, or heard, or
said in the house on Stink Alley—though he could have
experienced everything related here, for all of the major
facts are historically true.

As a young man, Elder William Brewster was in the
employ of Elizabeth's official minister, Sir William Davison. In Leyden, Brewster did indeed print a number of
books (especially Calderwood's *Perth Assembly,* as well
as his *De regimine Ecclesiae Scoticanae—Of the Gover-
nance of the Scottish Church*) at his Choir Alley
address. Smuggled into England and Scotland in wine
barrels, these books and pamphlets so infuriated King
James and his bishops that a manhunt was begun, in
England and in Holland, for the author and the printers
of these seditious works. Thomas Brewer was arrested
and closely questioned by the King; and Elder Brewster
became a hunted man, in hiding from April, 1619, until
the *Mayflower* sailed in September, 1620.

I have tried to show how dangerous—politically and

personally—it could be, in those days, to refuse to conform to King James's Church of England. Tremendously more dangerous, for example, than to burn the American flag today.

The insistence of the Scrooby Pilgrims upon choosing their own pastors was so radically democratic an action, and so challenging to royal authority, that it brought about not only great changes in religious worship, but later led to revolution and civil war in England, in the 1640s, and contributed to the spirit that led to revolution in America in 1776.

Of course the *Mayflower* Pilgrims had no inkling of this when they anchored in Provincetown harbor, on Cape Cod, on November 11, 1620; nor when they founded Plymouth six weeks later. They only knew they wanted to be "ye Lord's free people," and that they had dared to come to a dangerous New World, in search of "libertie."

They called themselves Saints, but we have come to call them Pilgrims; for in his famous book, *Of Plymouth Plantation,* Elder William Brewster's adopted son, Governor William Bradford, wrote: "So they lefte that goodly and plesante citie [Leyden], which had been ther resting place near 12 years; but they knew they were pilgrimes and looked not much on those things, but lift up their eyes to the heavens, their dearest cuntrie, and quieted their spirits."

Pastor Robinson never came to America; he died in Leyden in 1625, and was buried there in St. Peter's Church. Thomas Brewer was clapped in jail in England, for his radical beliefs, in 1624. Fourteen years later, still in prison, he died.

The Brewster family had a happier fate. They saw William Bradford, the orphan boy they had befriended, become the respected governor of Plymouth Colony. Mary Brewster (who died in 1627) lived to welcome her son Jonathan when he arrived in Plymouth, on the *Fortune,* in November, 1621; and her daughters, Patience and Fear, who followed on the *Anne,* in 1623. All of the Brewster children (except Wrastle, who died young) married here in the New World. And when Elder Brewster died, at 77 (in 1643), he could boast of fourteen grandchildren.

A final word about historical stereotypes, and the tricks the mind can play upon us when we try to force eras into separate compartments, for the sake of convenience. How easy it is to think of the Pilgrims only as contemporaries of the Stuart kings. It required repeated mental effort on my part to remember that many of the passengers on the *Mayflower* grew up in the Elizabethan age. William Brewster was a vigorous young man of twenty-two when the Armada sailed in 1588; he was the thirty-seven-year-old father of two children when old Queen Elizabeth died in 1603; he was forty-one when Jamestown was founded in 1607. And in 1616—three years before William Brewster began printing *Perth Assembly* on Stink Alley, and four years before the *Mayflower* sailed—William Shakespeare died.

Acknowledgments

In writing this book, I have drawn my material chiefly from four excellent books. They are: *Saints and Strangers,* by George F. Willison, Reynal & Hitchcock, New York, 1945; *The Story of the Pilgrim Fathers, 1606–1623 A.D., as told by Themselves, their Friends, and their Enemies.* Edited from the original texts by Edward Arber. Ward and Downey, Ltd., London, 1897; *Of Plymouth Plantation, 1620–1647,* by William Bradford, sometime Governor thereof, edited by Samuel Eliot Morison, Knopf, New York, 1952; and *The England and Holland of the Pilgrims* by Henry M. Dexter and Martin Dexter, Houghton, Mifflin & Co., Boston, 1905.

I should also like to thank for all their help Sylvia C. Hilton and the staff of the New York Society Library, where, for the most part, my research was done.

F.N.M.

Thanks to the Consulate General of the Netherlands for providing photographic research of the Robinson home in Leyden that was used as source material for the artwork on page 20.

R.Q.

About the Author

F. N. Monjo grew up in Stamford Connecticut and, as a child, acquired a lively sense of history. Within his own family he heard anecdotes of events going back to Civil War times. A graduate of Columbia University, for more than twenty years F. N. Monjo has been an editor specializing in children's literature. In addition, he is the author of more than twenty books for young readers, among them *Poor Richard in France,* and *Grand Papa and Ellen Aroon.* He lives in Manhattan with his wife, a first grade teacher, and their four children.

About the Artist

Robert Quackenbush has illustrated over sixty books and is the author/illustrator of twenty of his own books for young readers. In addition, his art has been exhibited at leading museums throughout the country. He resides in New York City with his wife and young son, Piet, who was named after the first Quackenbush ancestor to leave Leyden, Holland for America in the year 1632.

About the Book

The illustrations for this book were rendered in simulated woodcuts in the manner of the period via the scratch board technique. The text was set in Century Schoolbook and the display type is Century Schoolbook and Century Schoolbook Bold.